Good Night, Little Bear

Illustrated by Veronica Vasylenko

7373 North Cicero Avenue
Lincolnwood, Illinois 60712

Ground Floor, 59 Gloucester Place
London W1U 8JJ

ISBN-13: 978-1-4508-2993-9
ISBN-10: 1-4508-2993-7

Falling asleep, Little Bear,
is easier than it seems.

With bedtime hugs from those we love,
we slumber with sweet dreams.

Bedtime hugs for Little Turtle,
tucked inside a shell.

Bedtime hugs for Little Deer,

who cuddles in the dell.

Bedtime hugs for Little Fox,
In the middle of the night.

Bedtime hugs for Little Mouse,
who's had an evening bite.

Bedtime hugs for you, Little Bear,
and just like all the rest,

You'll soon be dreaming happy dreams
' cause hugging is the best!